Pony Party

by Kate Egan
illustrated by Carlo LoRaso

HarperFestival®
A Division of HarperCollins*Publishers*

Ponyville was quiet,
but it wouldn't be quiet for long.
The ponies were having a costume party at the Castle!

Wysteria was dressed as a hula dancer.
She hung a strand of colorful flowers around her neck.
She straightened her grass skirt.
Then she rushed to the Castle to finish the decorations.

Cotton Candy frosted one last cupcake for the party.
She kept her apron tied when she was finished.
Then she put on a chef's hat.
No one would be surprised by *her* costume!

Rainbow Dash looked just like a movie star!
She smoothed her hair.
She adjusted her sunglasses.
She was ready to go.

But not all of the ponies were ready.
Pinkie Pie stared at a big trunk full of dress-up clothes.
"What should I wear?" Pinkie Pie sighed.
"It's so hard to choose!"

Luckily, some of her friends were there to help.
Sparkleworks held up a tutu and twirled.
"You'd make a pretty ballerina," she suggested.
Pinkie Pie shook her head.

Sunny Daze asked, "How about a clown?"
She put a funny wig on Pinkie Pie.
Pinkie Pie couldn't see!
The three friends laughed,
but Pinkie Pie still didn't have a costume.

Soon the ponies found a glittery cloak in the trunk.
And then they found a horn.
Sparkleworks had a great idea.
"Pinkie Pie, you can be a unicorn!"

Pinkie Pie loved her costume.
She couldn't wait to get to the party.

At the Castle, sparkly balloons floated in the air.
Cotton Candy was serving cupcakes.
Some ponies were already dancing.

Pinkie Pie enjoyed looking at her friends' costumes.
Kimono fluttered by with big white wings.
She made a perfect angel.

Minty was dressed as a pony from outer space.
Her outfit was shiny and silvery.
Her antennae bounced when she danced.

Everyone said they loved Pinkie Pie's costume.
She was having the best time ever.

Then someone stepped on Pinkie Pie's cloak by mistake.
Now it had a big rip near the bottom.
"No one will notice," said Rainbow Dash.
But Pinkie Pie kept sneaking peeks at the tear.

As Pinkie Pie danced, she forgot about the tear.
She also forgot to look where she was going.
Pinkie Pie danced right into the punch bowl.

Her costume was soaked and her horn broke right in half!
She didn't look like a unicorn anymore.
She wasn't having fun anymore.
She felt like crying.

Sparkleworks winked at the other ponies.
Then she waved her wand over Pinkie Pie.
"Abracadabra," she said. "Alakazam!
Bring me a costume as fast as you can!"

Minty took off her antennae.
She put them on Pinkie Pie's head.
What were Pinkie Pie's friends up to?

Rainbow Dash offered her sunglasses.
Pinkie Pie put them on.

"Doesn't she look fabulous, ponies?" Rainbow Dash asked.
Pinkie Pie pretended to smile.
She still wished she had a costume.

But Pinkie Pie's friends weren't finished.
Kimono pinned her wings on Pinkie Pie.
Wysteria handed her a bunch of flowers.
Now Pinkie Pie did look like *something*.
She just couldn't think what it was.

Sunny Daze was dressed as a cheerleader.
She jumped in the air and shook her pom-poms.
"Three cheers for Pinkie Pie!
She's a lovely butterfly!"

Pinkie Pie looked at what she was wearing.
She smiled again—this time for real.
Her new costume was beautiful.
And with friends like these, she could fly anywhere.